CROSSWINDS PRESS, INC.
P.O. Box 683
Mystic, Connecticut 06355
crosswindspress.com

Printed in the United States of America

ISBN 978-0-9825559-1-0

10 9 8 7 6 5 4 3 2 1

Book design by Trish Sinsigalli LaPointe, LaPointe Design.
Old Mystic, Connecticut
tslapointedesign.com

Printed by The Racine Company
Brooklyn, Connecticut
racinecompany.com

Printed on environmentally friendly,
silk coated, acid-free, archival paper.

The Boomerang

BY CJ CONNOLLY
ILLUSTRATED BY LISA ADAMS

CROSSWINDS PRESS, INC.

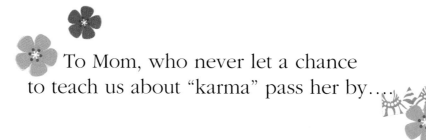

To Mom, who never let a chance
to teach us about "karma" pass her by…..

Prologue

This book is a continuation of the series that began with *Wil, Fitz and a Flea Named "T."* Mr. T is a wise old flea that has decided to help Wil learn a few of life's lessons while having fun along the way.

As might be expected, Mr. T has a lot of relatives who tend to visit more often than Fitz, Wil's dog, would probably like. They all bear names made up of letters (anywhere from one to twenty-three) that provide insight into their personality and the adventure to come. In this book, T's Australian cousin ZED helps unravel the mysteries of a boomerang. Enjoy!

It was a wonderful day…the sky was blue
Yet Wil was sitting 'round, wondering what to do.
No one else was outside 'cept Fitz and T…
And they were both sleeping under the big oak tree.

...GiddAY...

"Hey, Wil….or Gidday Mate should I say?
What you doin' out here? Do you want to play?"
Asked Ted the Australian, with his funny voice.
Wil liked him a lot….he was really quite nice!

As Wil and Ted chatted, Fitz's hair fluffed a bit
A fluff that moved from his tail to his hip…
Then on to the head of the sleepy old dog
But Fitz didn't notice…he was busy sawing logs!

Zed the Australian flea was on a vacation,
Traveling with Ted to many locations.
"Harumphhh" responded T as he woke from his nap.
"Who are you," he asked…he actually snapped!

"I'm your cousin Zed, though twice removed,
I've traveled far with Ol' Ted to see you!
My 'rents send their best, they couldn't make it...
To this far away place that's so close to Nantucket!"

"Are you sure we're related, you look kind of funny.
With that crazy hat…kind of like a small bunny!"
Said T as he looked over Zed his strange cousin,
On the lookout for others as fleas travel in dozens!

"Of course we're mates," said Zed with a smile,
"It's just that we've all been Down Under a while.
Here's a picture of your Australian family
Aunts, uncles, cousins and pets don't you see!"

"When I left them ZIP was the newest Aussie flea,
But now ZERO and ZILCH have joined the family!
My parents like patterns, like ZEBRA and ZOO,
Making naming us all a big job to do!"

"They might need a new letter if they've focused on Z,"
Said T with a smile as he strained to see…
What Ted had just pulled out from his pack…
A stick that he tossed…that came right back!

"It's a boomerang, mate…Ted loves the old things.
He loves to toss 'em…make 'em take wing."
Said Zed as Ted handed the 'boom to young Wil.
Who looked quite happy…he was actually thrilled!

Wil looked at the boomerang, then sized up Sir Ted,
Held out his arm and cleared his head….
He counted to three then tossed the thing..
But it didn't fly…no…it didn't take wing.

Wil mumbled and muttered and again gave it a wing,
Then ducked in surprise as he heard it go ZING!
It went past his ear and clipped Fitzy's head,
Fitz yelped just a little, then off he fled.

As he ran Wil could hear that tiny flea "T"
Yelling, "Stop Mr. Fitz before I count three!"
Mr. Ted then looked puzzled and wiggled his ears,
That seemed to happen lots when Mr. T was near.

Soon the lesson was over, at least so Wil thought,
Until Ted gave him a present, a gift he had brought.
Wil ripped open the wrapping then smiled quite brightly
"A boomerang! Hey thanks!" he said so politely.

"When you toss this boomerang you'll learn about life,"
Said Ted happily as he winked twice.
And while no one was watching Zed leapt to Ted's pack,
He was off to Australia…it was time to go back!

The party was over, they'd all gone home…
Leaving Wil, Fitz and T all alone…
Wil kicked at the dirt and tossed a few sticks,
To Fitz as he tried to teach the old dog new tricks.

Then he spotted the boomerang, the prize where it lay,
Just where he had left it when Ted went away.
Wil picked up that funny old curved piece of wood,
And tossed it quite hard from right there where he stood.

It didn't come back, though, it didn't even flutter,
As it dropped to the ground "Oh heck!" Wil did mutter.
He grabbed it again, he threw twice as hard,
The boomerang just plopped…right there in the yard.

Again and again and again he did fling it,
But not once did it fly, not a bit, no it didn't.
"Doggone, oh bother, oh heck, what's the matter…
I'm quitting right now, before I get even madder!"

With a flip of his wrist Wil gave it his best,
As he threw the boomerang out, far to the West.
As he turned on his heel and stomped off to the right,
"Duck" yelled out T....oh he cringed at the sight!

The boomerang was flying so fast it was hummin',
Right at Wil's head...he didn't see it coming!
BASH it did crash into Wil's curly locks...
And over he fell, surprised...quite in shock!

"OUCH!" shouted Wil. "I've been hit, I've been injured!"
He yelled it out loud, as he rubbed with his fingers.
"There's a lump on my head, who did this to me?"
Wil looked all around, then he looked down at T.

"Don't look at me, Wil" said Mr. T in a huff,
"I haven't done anything, but you've done quite enough!
In fact I've been thinking, have pondered you see…
'cause that boomerang is still quite a mystery to me."

"It seems to respond to one's heart not one's head,
It's a curious device you've been given by Ted.
Let's think aloud, Wil, let's talk you and me,
About this darn boomerang," squeaked Mr.T.

"Wil, what were you thinking as you tossed it about,
Were you so happy you wanted to shout?
Or was it in anger that you flung it away,
When it hit you so hard in the head this fine day?"

"It depends," said Wil, "As it often does,
On when you are asking and what is the buzz.
If I think on the two times it's come back to me,
AHA!!! I understand it, do you Mr. T?"

"Perhaps, Wil, somehow, yes now it makes sense,
You've gotten what you've given….no more and no less.
When you toss it out lightly with a smile in your heart,
It comes gently back…back where it did start."

"That's right, Mr. T! I can see it, I can!"
"When I try to force flying it falls in the sand.
But if I toss softly and think happy thoughts,
The boomerang goes, then returns, to this spot."

"What's more, if I'm right, it's as clear as a bell,
When I fling it in anger, I don't do very well.
At best it drops PLUNK like a rock on the ground,
At worst it comes back…and hits me quite sound!"

As Wil thought it over, he picked up his "boom,"
He thought happy thoughts and whistled a tune…
Then oh so softly he let go, let it fly…
It traveled so gently, so high in the sky….
And floated back to Wil, as he whispered "Hi!"

As Ted had predicted Wil learned quite a lesson,
About how what you do comes on back as a blessin'
Or a curse if that's what you gave out at the start,
Goodness only comes back to a warm, loving heart....